FUNNYBONES

Janet and Allan Ahlberg

SCHOLASTIC BOOK SERVICES

NEW YORK · TORONTO · LONDON · AUCKLAND · SYDNEY · TOKYO

This is how the story begins.
On a dark dark hill
there was a dark dark town.
In the dark dark town
there was a dark dark street.
In the dark dark street
there was a dark dark house.
In the dark dark house
there was a dark dark staircase.
Down the dark dark staircase
there was a dark dark cellar.
And in the dark dark cellar . . .

There was a big skeleton,
a little skeleton and a dog skeleton.

One night the big skeleton
sat up in bed.
He scratched his skull.
"What shall we do tonight?" he said.
"Let's take the dog for a walk,"
said the little skeleton.
"And frighten somebody!"
"Good idea!" the big skeleton said.

So the big skeleton,
the little skeleton
and the dog skeleton
left the dark dark cellar,
climbed the dark dark staircase
and stepped out into the dark dark street

They walked past the houses
and the shops.
They walked past the zoo
and the police station.
They went into the park.

The big skeleton scratched his skull.
"What shall we do now?" he said.
"Let's play on the swings,"
said the little skeleton.
"And throw a stick for the dog –
and frighten somebody!"
"Good idea!" the big skeleton said.

WHAT
SHALL WE DO
NOW?

The big skeleton and the little skeleton
played on the swings.
They threw a stick for the dog.

Suddenly something happened.
The dog skeleton chased the stick,
tripped over a park bench,
bumped into a tree –

and ended up as a little pile of bones.

"Look at that!" the big skeleton said.
"He's all come to pieces.
What shall we do now?"
"Let's put him together again,"
the little skeleton said.
So the big skeleton
and the little skeleton
put the dog skeleton together again.
They sang a song while they did it.

THE TOE BONE'S CONNECTED TO THE — FOOT BONE!

THE FOOT BONE'S CONNECTED TO THE — LEG BONE!

THE LEG BONE'S CONNECTED TO THE — HIP BONE!

THE HIP BONE'S CONNECTED TO THE — BACK BONE!

Then they got mixed up.
"Is that a toe bone?"
the little skeleton said.
"Where does this one go?"
said the big skeleton.

When they had finished, the big
skeleton said,
"That dog looks a bit funny to me."
"So he does," said the little skeleton.
"We've got his tail on the wrong end –
and his head!"
"Foow!" said the dog skeleton.

At last the dog was properly
put back together again.
The big skeleton and the little skeleton
sang another song.

The big skeleton scratched his skull.
"That reminds me," he said.
"We forgot to frighten somebody!"
"Let's do it on the way home, then,"
said the little skeleton.
"Good idea!" the big skeleton said.

So the big skeleton,
the little skeleton and the dog skeleton
left the dark dark swings,
went out into the dark dark town –
and tried to frighten somebody.

The trouble was, there wasn't anybody.
Everybody was in bed.
Even the policemen in the police station
were in bed.
Even the animals in the zoo!
Of course, the *skeleton* animals
were awake.

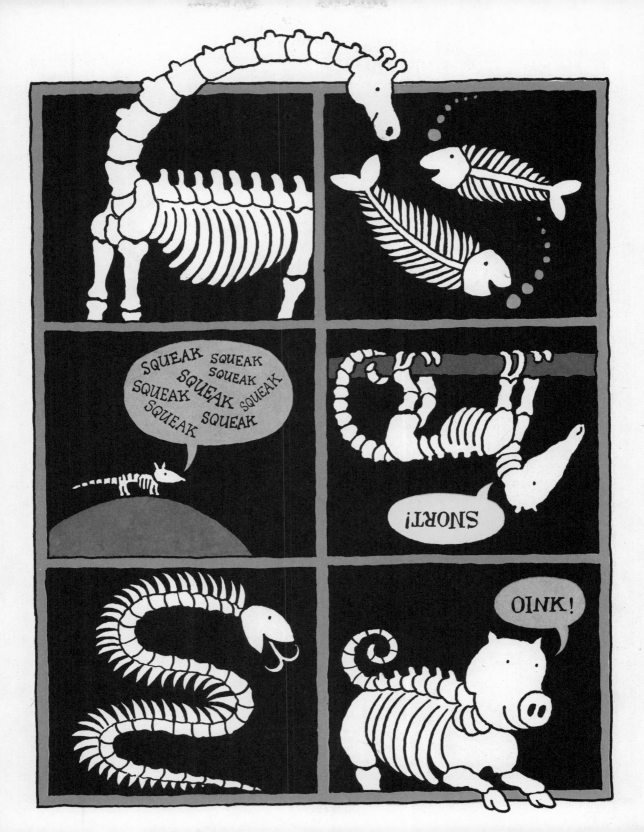

"Let's have a ride on the elephant skeleton," the little skeleton said.
"Let's have a word with the parrot skeleton."
The big skeleton scratched his skull.
"Let's . . . keep out of the way of the crocodile skeleton," he said.

The little skeleton scratched *his* skull.
"Let's frighten each other!" he said.
"That's better than nothing!"
"Good idea!" the big skeleton said.

So after that the big skeleton
frightened the little skeleton,
the little skeleton
frightened the big skeleton,
the big skeleton and the little skeleton
frightened the dog skeleton,
and the dog skeleton frightened them.

They hid round corners
and frightened each other.
They climbed up lamp posts
and frightened each other.
They jumped out of dustbins
and frightened each other –

all the way home.

And that is how the story ends.
On a dark dark hill
there was a dark dark town.
In the dark dark town
there was a dark dark street.
In the dark dark street
there was a dark dark house.
In the dark dark house
there was a dark dark staircase.
Down the dark dark staircase
there was a dark dark cellar.
In the dark dark cellar
some skeletons lived.

They still do.

THE END

0-590-32547-7

Copyright © 1980 by Allan Ahlberg and Janet Ahlberg. All rights reserved. This edition published by Scholastic Book Services, a division of Scholastic Inc., 730 Broadway, New York, NY 10003, by arrangement with Greenwillow Books, a division of William Morrow & Company, Inc.

12 11 10 9 8 7 6 5 4 3 2 1   10   2 3 4 5 6/8
Printed in the U.S.A.   09